JURIST

TRAGEDY OF CAPER

SUMEET KUMAR

ISBN 979-888629093-6

Sumeet Kumar

Sumeet Kumar , A adult who experiences many phases of love in his life , get broked many times , stands up every time and keep moving to the next phases of the life.In reality he is a writter as well as singer (as a hobby). Very exciting and interesting fact about him is that he is author of New era i.e. he starts his journey of writing at the age when he was going to schools to get the study . His some famous works i.e. Maturity Of Love (Genre - Love),Privacy For Dream (Genre - Middle Class), Army Squad ofLove

(Genre- The Seperation of Army Love), 5 Days of Love(Genre- Temporarily Love), Th e Endearment Of Love(Genre - Historical Era Of Love), Social Destruction Indo-Pak (Genre - The Story of The Love At The Time Of Division Of India And Pakistan), Middle Class Soul (Genre - The Dreams of Middle Class), The Accursed Kanatpur (Genre -The Horrific Story Of A Village), Wrong Number (Genre -The Suspenseful Physco Killer Story), The Secrecy OfDeadly Midnight (Genre - The Suspense About a Crime),Fragile Religious Of Death (Genre- The Death Of A TrustfulPerson), Nature Vs Science (Genre - The Future Battle Between Nature And Science In A Horrific Way), Generic Man (Genre - The Dream of I.I.T), The Unconsious 12 Hours(Genre - The Illusion At Stage Of Comma), The StrangeBurden (Genre - The Burden Of Love) , Her Existence (Genre- The Female Pain In The Society) , Jockstrap Prize (Genre -The True Story Of A National Athlete) , H Man [Hindi] (Genre - Superhero Tragic Story), H Man [English] (Genre - Superhero Tragic Story) , Maturity Of Love [Englsih] (Genre - Love) and many more are available on various geners on the offcial platform of **Amazon, Flipkart and Notionpress**. You can buy them from there.

Contents

Acknowledgements

Aman Kumar

Special Thanks to **Aman Kumar** who worked so hard in the preparation of this book. He has continually put with my passive voice, omission of words, and late night calls. You have be en wonderful. Thanks to him for his precious time in reviewing proposals , individual chapters and early drafts, along with his suggestions on the applicability of the material to the world.

I

INVISIBLE WAY

Somebody had heard that love makes the walls of
protection which cannot be broken, for some it becomes
that love to protect someone else, which no one can erase.
Nor is it love, it is a habit to give people a footless silence,
which they themselves can never take away from

themselves. God always thinks about him, cares for him and says nothing in return, what is love called love undefined Has any human witness ever asked what condition are you in undefined Has it ever been asked whether you are right or not undefined love Not as much as the lights, I have felt her love in the public when she was with me, I am neither Devdas nor any Romeo, they forget all the times and their love also because everyone has the habit of support these days. Why can't you bear your own silence who has prepared for you that grave which you don't even need ? Why do you say returning to his life, in whose life there is not even a small true glimpse of your existence. It is not a matter that I have broken his love, I have got some kind of risk because in things I I haven't even thought about it, it's not that I didn't have love, I also played the same passion that others are doing till now, that too to add to a relationship, when people in life started giving themselves to someone else, then of course Let this society go that it is far away from you, it is such a destination whose dreams can be seen by being involved in such a great gathering, feet that too like a dream because his vision is very different from your thinking, every witness these days says that I should be with you. I am not infatuated with beauty, this is my love for you, these lamps are like a dream in the night's dream I have acquired the love of giving space, so that witness will listen to your every word, then it will be tormented. Why are they including prison in their part undefined Nowadays when people used to break in love, they say that I am trying hard enough that my feet can't separate it from itself. Every single thing has shone in my mind that I can't separate myself from it even after saying it I don't know why this is happening with me undefined feet A glimpse of the evening I kill the love of living, nothing is happening, I can't bear my own silence now, when she tells me by refusing to respect me that I can no longer be with you, then I do my own existence too Why can't I feel the pain like his conversation? Why do I always enough in front of him? Undefined Why do I plot to spoil every single moment of my life on my own? I find the reason for his being, I know that I can request to be separated from him How to do it if it was only a matter of time, then let it go to its memories also it has the ability to live in such a way that I can neither hurt myself nor can I narrate the lane close to myself, I ask to run and his friends From and to his existence, he would have become so distant that even those women of him could never find me. Each one sees his own importance, say whether it is a relationship, be it an animal, your choice is a loved thing, even if it is time to come, a ghoul also shows its Ehmite, that too the teacher whose gathering I don't wish for, never accepts this story. Neither me nor any other witness, because it is a matter of good faith, justice, which everyone says is a habit, whose power now everyone should not even prove someone's love in the feet because its attachment is only illusion. There is such a thing that when people are right then we try to understand them wrong and when people are wrong we make it a habit to understand them right. There is also a fascination, in fact, there are many mysteries behind it which will be written in the gift of pages today. These tears which flow for each other, these lamps are also very much related to the mystery and the power is connected to the extent like a In fear and in anger, I tell everyone to make everyone aware of those candles in the festival that there is no gift of love, these are the best intentions of the game, thinking of which you are very far away from humanity

Mini love conversation absolutely Human is like thinking which is for a moment only because human being has created humanity, not everyone has the passion to walk on foot, not everyone in our community, these people can fight for even a piece of land by taking boundaries regarding religions. Feet is not at all for humanity, every witness from his life says that everything should be better in his life and he should not have to face any kind of trouble and this bail is also right and why not be undefined to live on his own For today's people, if I were in their place, I would also think that such a thinking is undefined. The two conversation were very well said and I say that whatever is included in the festival today, why is it my silence, they should also listen carefully to my batis, I will not give a shadow of mystery to the lamps of the witness, why even his words Come in front of a big gathering because he had played something like this game and you all know that when a player plays his game better then he should be praised, well, I should give some light to those baton feet now he had said that No one destroys us in the world, it is our own saying that gives us the reason to destroy and what you love for me is right, the feet on your part, there is no pride in my part anymore Now there is no difference, now I say to walk on my own way. I said it right Seeker does feet, human beings also do this, I had never thought that because the day he left me, my feelings for him have already been killed for him. it will come back if a sex requests you that he has forgotten her and he has now moved on in his life, then all the things he said in front of you are made only with shoes intentions because if this thing were true So that witness only ever mentions about male infidelity, has forgotten in his alpha suhe toh ok why not to make his lamps famous in front of anyone else, if you have given your passion to move forward in life, then repeat it again and again What's the benefit of a boy's life? It's not a good thing in the life of a boy because the lights of the society remind him all the time that your life is also a gift, your family, which you will have to take care of when you grow up from childhood till he Until he attains the age of old age, he is made to realize all the time that you grow up. To take care of the condition of the house, to do a good job, to be the support of mother and father, to get the sister married, to look after yourself, to read your younger daughter-in-law too, these things are not wrong about a family, of course we have to do this It is our duty and these things are also right, our feet are also such that we can keep a enough inside ourselves because if we have the habit of doing left, then those troubles take China from us, this is the duty that everyone has realized from us. I have given these feet, some people are only applicable to feet, I mean it is not applicable to the entire community of boys because there are many girls who do this work and make boys better, I am not promoting any one community. Nor am I slamming anyone, Bash, who has realized life, I am telling him to call it a debate. Well it is not just baton, this is the truth that some people come to me, they never adopt their feet in their life. Because the love of two moments makes them so cowardly that they even lost their fate to the society, there is not much power in life to save some witnesses. To go ahead and move forward, for the sake of which he has lost everything, he also has feet to give him two moments of happiness I see with my eyes, this toh enough is that of the human world, in which every single day a person is destined to be liberated in those flames. To get, we have to say party to lose a lot and if we want to get rid of any pain from the pond, then a witness will have to make a habit of it, because the happiness that is lost in life will never come back, the feet that happiness It is going to come in the future, he should try to make himself worse or else he may not know that he will ever come again in the journey. Well, even the games of pronounciation can force a person to be a slave to someone, it is its incomplete Never thought in life there are such high accidents which are just like happiness, which do not need to hurt themselves. The reason is not known, nor does that pond support us at the right time, but to say so, now the whole festival has been given a lot of work on the feet, so I am going to share the moments of my life, which I myself have never loved alone. I didn't help my feet, maybe now that time's pain has also increased and my pain has increased a bit, so I have demanded the respect of myself long ago, so it is a request to stay with me in the journey. undefined

"That decree has been sent by God to me, in which the way of my death is very clearly written (2) Accidently i tried to erase that decree but suddenly a news comes out that on that day there will be a mairrage of the cheater who brokes my heart.
That is very heartless because I do not understand my condition, I express my sorrow every time.
But i think , Now she doesn't understand me, beyond this Even if I agree, what should I do? She is so beautiful about infidel but unable to understand the feelings of my heart."

II

LOVE IN SECTION

It takes a whole life to ride a relationship, only two moments are enough to break it, the love of life itself never takes the foot of any pabarbari because its rudeness is always loyal to itself. Many people meet each other, share, make relationships and request hate in a single moment, feet never separate from each other, say why they hate each other a lot, even if people say this in anger Give that I don't ask to see him in front of my eyes anymore, he doesn't like me, the very next day the same witness again makes new walls of hatred in his memory, if he intends to go away from someone, then he wants to go closer to him. Why make nature his share of happiness Why enough always requests to find himself in his friends undefined Those who have broken for some reason know that if even many small cracks in a relationship prove the reason for leisure, then they Never had love for each other, all these shoes are intentions, in reality in today's world I have to say some dreams, those who have troubled me for a long time, I never asked for this bailout, that give me some right place in the happy gathering of silence where many people are missing like me, before connecting with her every single moment she was aware The compulsion of my feet without my own pain was such that even the wastage of a couple of moments began to make me fall in love, even today, if she is seen somewhere in front of my eyes, then I ask myself the question whether there is any beautiful thing too. Can my displeasure hurt? History is a testament to the fact that till date no one has got true love and even if it is one sided, it is not only one sided, because on the other side only the world of deception is visible, which Neither can he see with his eyes nor can he ever feel it, it was not even his fault. Who did not get even a small amount of her right, because in her happiness I never saw the bailout of my sorrow, enoughwas such a story. Gone in the world for a long time when even his enmity seemed to me infatuated. I can't find the right reason where I can tell myself that it is wrong, it says that the love of a good person can never speak to anyone, even if it is someone's infidelity, then that too to him. Man accepts his share of time, if the desire to put his heart is wrong, then how can that love be right? Am behind him? Why am I thinking about bashushi all the time? With a heart that tries to forget him forever, I don't know what I did for him foot and it was a reality That I did all that for both of us who can keep our relationship safe, I have written the story of pain to a great extent, my part has written foot bailout journey. Oh, I have decided now that my anger has asked me to forget myself, that too in the support of his friends, I recommend every moment to love once again, what I spent with him, to do those things again. I say that what I did to him, I tell him to go away without any promises that he made to me, this is not a story only for both of us, this is my whole life, what I believed in him, that too not for a moment but my death Till .Vaidik Verma, that witness who got every happiness in the world, in his luck, he was wrapped in the gift of sorrow, that means, in return for whatever he wanted in life, he only showed pain all the time, forgot many accidents. I have seen many accidents, even with my eyes, I never thought that the shadow of those accidents would one day become the gift of my death. And if by mistake it changes for a few moments, then one day it becomes the destruction of the human witness, who has lost his own love in those moments. Whose walls are also slaves of silence. So my story begins with such a ruin, whose name was Riddhi Kalra, a girl who was beautiful with her feet, she would have started with only two things and those two things feet Let me tell the end as well, those two things were quite out of the status of a common man, because his love could only be pure, whose thinking would have been like happiness, in the same way, let me tell the suggestion of the gathering where we both met for the first time. Name, Then it was a conversation where even her thinking would have been sweeter than love and ending also means the world of Agra Shah Jahan and Mumtaz where they could never be one despite each other, meaning their death shone their fate. The fate of the idol never mixed them again, well, it is their love for their daughters, that too for each other, why do we let them become the third person in the middle undefined, they also love each other with love. So in my story Ridhi Kalra is the person who gave me happiness in the gift of sorrow and I have said these things earlier also. The witness in me who got happiness, feet are wrapped in the gift of sorrow, so how could this saying of mine be different from the other, in the same way, the story of both of us is not too long, feet is not too short, not even mean to say average because my life is also average And our love also means average when I met her for the first time, I thought that day, that girl, whose love I have in protecting tradition, I would be destined, never thought that it would be the reason that my pain narrates. Will increase the fold even more, I have told my life on average because I used to belong to a lower middle class family and the whole world knows its condition means two moments of happiness and "life's sorrow that too two rupees tea and Work sent together" Means my father tell all the time that our community is like this because their life has also not been anything special, neither he was the son of Ambani nor the relatives of Tata, what is the happiness in their life, what is their happiness, see them till today. No, well, let me meet my father, who is none other than the head of our house, whose name is Ajay Verma, such a mystery and hope that these conversations will remain only among us, so to say, Papa is the real head of the whole house. strange secret belongs to our mother who is none other than our small right world, she is the great happiness and she is the root that has kept us all connected, similarly the name of our world is Usha Verma, who is the favorite of all my happiness. Well, the breed of my family does not matter because I have not mixed the two friends of my house, who are my brothers and sisters and the precious gems of my small right world, in which I love myself more than my own. Younger sister Kiriti Verma and my brother Mridul Verma This is not only my family but it was the whole world about which I have said a lot of work because the bailout of time does not go to waste and if every dose of pain that I have suffered in my body, if it works, then perhaps that truth will never come out, which I have spent many times in my life. It is kept inside, the great thing about some stories is that they never end and the story of both of us was similar because I had tried hard enough that we both never met. Sister-in-law turned out to be unfaithful at the same time, which mixed us both again where we had separated from each other, I had even imagined that you would never get back to me because my shadow was too far away from me, that too Shimla In such a beautiful world where the exhibition of pain was completely oblivious, like my friends. By ending the relationship, its nib never ends. Peach is mad, always says that he is a fool Before telling my full story, the last few words that I want to say, love, if it is not old, then it is never forgotten because with time its fears also become our habit. 2013 Sat. John Academy Agra A school where beauty was his education, I mean knowledge of it was his beauty, most of the time when we are children, we think about cartoons, it is about a toy, my feet are all enough It was different, maybe one thing should not happen, let me tell you that the one who has compulsions in his house, he gets the phase of his motherhood very early in his childhood because the principle of the world is the locality in which we live, we consider it as our home. And the condition of my house and my love were the only flaws, that too after being born in a lower middle class family of money, people even think that why did the child take birth after all, if it was a boy, to a large extent he If she takes her feet as a girl, then dowry studies and many more surgeries are such things which have unnecessarily changed in the understanding, the condition of my house was also like this at the time when my father lost his job, so our condition at the same time. They were very spoiled, till they were two, their world was like the Taj Mahal, whose walls were rusted, yet that world He was famous for his feet, what was the news to him that the reason for improving his condition would get worse when I came to his world, the day I was born, he did not think that a happiness would come and because of happiness, he would go away because only in me The reason for his bad condition is that my father was a clerk in the bank and as soon as he entered his world, he had become a criminal, in the eyes of everyone, he was punished for such a crime that he had ever done. Did not mean that neither mother nor father ever told about the accident of theft, nor did father ever make them famous in my mind, no father says that even his evil shadow is above his son's feet. The incidents of the past, due to which his entire world went to China from him in a single day, were blamed on me because he himself had been blamed for his feet. The work has not been done, I have said that our condition was bad were broken and the courage of my house was my mother who never let them break. Regardless. Father's bank balance was very good with our year's earnings, we could neither think of it nor our hope till the extent of ever pouch husband means daughter of a very rich family, if I say normally, you must be thinking that If she was anti-rich then that school would also be very expensive and I asked how every time a scholarship bell was rang in the school, in which it was clearly written that whoever will pass the written examination of scholarship, we will get it in our school. Will teach until he graduates, even though my luck was upset, my feet were with me every step of the way, then what was the dream that Papa had seen for me, I was too peach to fulfill them And when the scholarship bell rang, I had passed the written exam by using the form undefined and after that, the foot of it was also a big deal. She was like from me because even after this there were many ability tests in which I had failed, yet they refused to give me a seat and I didn't even know the reason for this, but after a few days the news came that I The co-school has selected him again undefined What was happening in my life for a long time, I was not aware of anything, it was he who first came out of the conversation and later he called them, why did they come to know later? That he refused to take me to school because the accidents of my father's past had become a stain for my future, had become such an accident whose nature was to destroy me, he said that he was the one Can't give a seat to a boy whose father is a chur, he is a criminal How many times did he humiliate himself to plead for the future of his son, that too for me, he presented himself in front of him. The words have been erased that today when I think of those candles, I do not want to erase myself, why I asked for apologies undefined why I went weak undefined I would probably never know if I could not listen to her and her mother's candles secretly. He had said that now happiness has come in the house, we have become adamsson of the house. Feed me sweets in John's academy Miss Verma was very happy in the day because I had no information about the mystery, I was so happy because of the debate that I was all I will show myself with hardwork and become a successful person by hardwork, as my father says, my mother was also informed about the bottles because her husband came in front of someone else in a crowded gathering, that too only for me. For the son who had only seen happiness, the time had fallen, I had forgotten everything in my own eyes, when the truth had come in front of my eyes, at the time my studies were my disease and my hope to move forward and mother gave me Didn't even tell the time, that enoughwas happy to see me, he explained to his father for a long time about the things. And at last he hugged and said so much that let's eat food, it is too late. To be honest, my pen has run out. Can't let go because the gathering of sorrows, he didn't include me even though I would have included him in my happiness in my feet. I had not seen rote in front, say no matter how bad our condition may have been, for the first time I had seen tears in the eyes of a person, who had donated my happiness for me. I have heard these words that in order to get the love of a true heart, it is necessary to have a true heart too.

self stigma enough used to separate himself from his world so much that because of me, my father had got a new world to say never to bear all this again, this day I was filled with hatred and someone's arguments He used to say to ruin them, say that why should he be in any way, the reason behind him was only because of my dreams, because of my dreams, a human being folded his hands in front of him, who never interrupted his faith, that toh some people There were those who showed the sight of ruin in the gathering of happiness, I don't know these words, I have said it with my words, even though I may not have said it, yet I say that the love of a human being brings ruin for him every time. I can't make the other witness feel like saying that no matter how difficult that road may be, I didn't want to know the past of my family and neither did I I had never spoken wrong to my father, because I know that the witness did not leave his family even in the worst of circumstances, how can he win his faith for a little money, how can he separate his own love from his own self? A father does not work for a superhero because when we keep every wish of the world in the shadow of our dreams, then later he will see them in the color of dreams. Decorates what we call father The next day I went to St.John's Academy, so all my people were very different, meaning the human nature was in them, the feet were in a different way, which nothing else is called pride, that foot was no one alive, I thought all were dead because I saw my eyes Whenever the swirl belongs to mine enough was heard filtering the money and also the arc of richness.

""if there was a measuring machine for measuring someone's possession then the capacity of a poor would have been very high Because their hard work is clearly reflected in their love. . Even after burning his own hope, that father raised me , I have seen mother's love but that father's fingers have also handled me How can I forget the pain of whose silent lights have made me ride in happiness I am blessed that I have taken care of myself in the shadow of a father. ""

III
JOURNEY BEGINS

It is recommended that today I should say everything, I have given a little work, so I say to start my gathering, where its fanna was famous. Only I had heard that every day I have seen it with my own eyes, today I tell everyone to say something and those things are that if you are walking on one floor, then no matter how many problems come in its way, why do you ever come in your way? Steps take the mat behind him because when a traveler decides a destination, then his happy time ends for some other destination and he says that neither the old friends ever come back nor old accidents ever come back to anyone. The feet are repeated in the gathering, my gathering was already wasted, so now what right new ruin was going to come in my part, which I am proudly proud of in Gujarat. The most laughable and very beautiful girl of the academy, behind whom all the boys of the male academy were beyond the shadows like: Somebody the Eiffel Tower See, the feet were not even wrong in their place because a person runs after only two things in life, first wealth and secondly, the donation of someone's body and maybe even in both ways, I was not different from both the ways if the other people's love was in love,If other people were famous in love at that time, then there was work in that too, I also jumped to death by destroying someone else's feet and fulfilling the sayings and ponds of my frog because a person can forget his words, feet can never forget those sages in whose shadow he spent many nights like this Those who are made with the gusto of peace, I am talking about no one else but God, to whom I have mantained everything, that means, my father was silent during the debate even after knowing every fact, because he could not see his eyes at the right time. I knew that he would never reveal anything to himself because he could not see his son in trouble and I had given him so much trouble during that time that I myself did not even know how to make him angry with him. If I had wasted time, I would never have been successful in my purpose, where on one hand, all the boys of the Academy, Ridhi Kalra Whee feet were behind the people, there were some people who had a lot of trouble with me and maybe they used to give trouble to me somewhere, they were aware that they were a raw common society, they were quite sure of their principles and someone from a local I didn't have value and I was local, before hurting me, I gave him such trouble that he had forgotten the value of himself, know that a local person's skill is that he can hold everything and also undefined Can Perry then average in my story, to give them back what they were thinking to do with me, I returned them with care in undefined, so let's all show you a little bit of mishap I'll give it, before that let me tell you something else that the boys of every group were behind me, why they felt undefined I don't know the leg is undefined, the pain was enough for them because of me because undefined

"CONVERSATION"

"**ADHIR** : *Oye fresh listen here undefined undefined impatient who is the best boy in school and also a good player on the football pitch, there was no better defender and attacker than this, he says that those who have specialty, they do not do anything bad and there is no evil in it I was confident that no one can beat me in my field and whoever he is calling, it is none other than me undefined*

VAIDIK : *yes tell me !*

ADHIR : *I am a senior, by talking to your respect, your father has not taught you how: we talk to you elders undefined He says that you should never put your hands on your feet without burning, and he made a bigger mistake than that. I had kept my feet, I know all of you must be feeling a little*

different about these lamps.
VAIDIK: *Sikhya toh hai respect karna feet not*
like you. **"**

Whatever happened after this should not happen and I should not do such things to him, there is a reason behind this too Which is called VPR in good words and it is VPR where the cost of hard work used to end with happiness and feet Well let's first get a little nervous who has screwed me when I told him to give side now because even though I am a scholar was foot told him this thing, he knew that I was a local too and there is no problem of local, keep him in whatever climate he will live and he will also take heat, then what was the group of all the rich children, they all gathered together I got up and started trying to climb on me, I mean, trying to fill me, his wish would have been fulfilled at the same time, when a man tried to kill me from the group of people, I raised my hand and gave him so much bind and leave the factor of fear that no other person has come from this group, these things must have seemed a bit filmy, I know what to do, because it is true because he No normal prisoner was a father, after all a local had killed him and the little one of the local prisoner also affects like a blessing of God, then what was it when this accident happened, in a short time his parents came and meant to save them. Teachers have come to their feet, one thing is still surprising that they have not said anything, meaning they have not said anything about who beat them up was his parents were not a common man, he was a boy of some rubbish, when the ability of a local matches with any condition, then no matter what is in front, he does not leave him, I remember the name of the boy as well. No, still everyone was saying at the time that Roshan was undefined

Rocky) Means two names of a boy, why these two were different so much confusion why undefined when I am present, I will tell you after all the whole school has a topic foot talk at the time Then the topic was nothing new bash everyone was saying that a fresh ne rocky toh pir diya, even toh they have not even made memes. Both of me have feet on the soil networking sites and I knew that their ego is much bigger than my thinking and they will definitely take revenge for all of them, so I was ready beforehand, Jung also has a specialty that he never fought himself. And if by mistake even the heart becomes sick, then life makes us stand with such a mortal foot where we, even with ourselves, become sick at the same time, the witness in the world whose heart and mind are the same. I am so that witness can overcome all difficulties and can remain in every condition, my thinking was very different because at the time someone else had done such a magic on my feet that I had become my own raqeeb. At that time something happened that at the time when there was a fight with the power group, at that time Riddhi Kalra was present, who saw everything with her beautiful eyes and at that time she was fed up with me, what is it that is undefined, now everyone must be thinking well It's a farce later, man was love for me at the time and maybe somewhere for him I did not think that we will ever meet each other I and Khavish also didn't do anything special at the time because I used to ask to bring back the lost respect of my father and I would do nothing for him in the past. Even saying is not different because thinking of it only strengthens the walls of hatred, about which we never think about, what do I know that the hatred which I have been trained in, can also bring back the lost respect of my father. For Lane, she will make me fall in her own eyes that I will never be able to tell her to meet my eyes, I used to argue to bring her happiness back I didn't know. Well after all, my ruin had started and I really knew my feet, he says that we will become famous without the abuses of death. I had become a target in the group and tell me what was the group's too, then what was it, they tried a lot to ask me a little, every time I climbed the ladder of success. He should have studied climbing and said that he should study in sports because there were two reasons in which he could try to defeat me and even try to ask me small feet, his luck was not so good even when he could beat my hard work. In life, you achieve some success, don't say why it is not in something, then from time to time, I am a habit of the same thing, and it is also the beginning of wastage, time and fate is never a slave of any witness. It's a matter of keeping these things fixed within me and at that time it was very difficult for me to keep these things in my mind. There was also the need of a player whose defending skills would blow the senses of the people in front and those who were our opponents at the time were from the National Unity Academy, who not only had unity in their work but also had a lot of unity in their work. And even before this, he had defeated St John Academy many times in his own sports and many other academy were in trouble.There was a lot of lack of potential in them, then at that time a new boy is entered in our academy, who had challenged the captain of St

John Academy as soon as he arrived. Sameer rathore undefined International Player) Foot this thing no one knew at the time, he is an international player and at that time the captain of St John was also an international player, which means that the fight of the war was not with each other but with himself. Hi status seh thi means Ayu Rajput (who was the captain of our football team and on the other hand Sameer rathore whose skill was the best and these things we came to know when something happened undefined which should not have happened at good time because good time trial) The mode was turned on by everyone means these rules of sports future were that any outside player can take the place of any one of us if he belongs to the academy, and even if not, then these rules will apply. There was such a race in the whole school that half of the time half the boxes studied in half the whole academy. I had left it because this match was very important for our academy because its winning prize was something like this and that winning prize was that the team which wins the match can replace the other academy that means they are male. Every single piece of the academy can be enslaved by itself, simple language, so the academy which will lose the match will be given to the academy that wins by doing China from their hands, that means their entire academy and their children too. Now it is only There was not a match but there was a battle that too about the captaincy, which was requested at the time of both of them. And on the other hand Sameer used to say to play the match because he had old problems with Ayu in the international match because before this Ayu had defeated Sameer many times, you all must be thinking that this my story is like some morr foot. In the previous meaning, where and where has come Match undefined And I have said in all Incident say, this is my own failure, it is not news, it is the condition due to which my luck had completely changed. Everyone was surprised to see that all the students of Sat John Academy and many of his friends also happened to such an accident that for the first time in the same match, Sameer defeated Ayu 4-1, which was the biggest victory for him. And on the other hand, the biggest defeat of age, these batis were not worth believing, foot everything happened in front of our eyes, so we have to trust even without saying so, only one time was found in mercury before this, when Ahir fight with me on that time It happened that he was the senior of all of us and there was also such a boy whose thinking of happiness used to start and he did not even know the end of his feet, the day my ahir Why did he support me because neither he was my friend nor we had ever met each other before then why did he do this undefined I was blown away that the Beast of St John Academy has lost his war, he is also a non-noob player, I had already said that it was not just a match but a Jung and between them who hate each other very much Undefined Why am I telling you all about their hair? a new way come to my life and it is also belongs to my Story have are different undefined When this thing started reverberating in the whole academy that age was defeated by a non noob player then what was the friendship never fascinated anyone, it was a special day that means ushi's friends are no longer with him Because it is the tradition of the world, people always like to be behind a person who always has success, not the one who is better than his heart That he has been defeated by a nonub palye, who makes a lot of money from him. Even after all in the field, he did not consider himself a failure, even while leaving, he had said only one thing to the complete Academy that if I have failed today, it does not mean that my academy has also failed, I should say ssid ot was not possible. There should be no other debate in my place, as much as my academy, the academy that my entire family had been talking about. From a quick glance, the legend of any anger gets worse when I heard this thing, I could not believe that the age which I have seen many times playing in front of my eyes and the claws of the opponents of other teams. His fate has seen a delay in his part, that age has been lost to a non-noob player who has been playing for only a few months, meaning how undefined how did he go undefined is there any animosity between many people? He lost the matches himself won, he too alone. Then how did it happen undefined was undefined How can I do ohh undefined I had forgotten that only money was the rule and money can be bought and how did I forget this? Those who promise to fulfill the hope of your dreams, they will play the vows, in the end, their legend compels us to lose our fear that we men start looking for the darkness, whose dreams we have never even seen with our closed eyes. The day enmity broke out, the feet had become so much that despite being in front of the real people, no one could see his true self. He has lost his age, Samir has lost his feet, this is not a reality, this is just a show, what ayur had done at the time, that too to save himself, what was the reason for the legs undefined and why did he do this undefined I was told that what I want to reveal in front of all of you is undefined

CONVERSATION

"**AYU**: *O Vedic! I want to say something to you .*
VAIDIK : *Say yes, I'm sorry for your harem, I didn't know at all that you're going to lose the match, actually I can't believe that he can beat you sometime undefined*
AYU : *yes , You have hurt me but i have no regrets i say bash so much that my academy should win the debate and my team bash get a good captain who is even better and maybe Sameer is right for this mujseh is better he undefined*

__VAIDIK__ : Better than you undefined I am seeing a dream in this place, in my place there is such a reality in front of me that I do not want to say that you are the best player of our academy and also the best captain, how could you be better under undefined undefined is undefined

__AYU__ : anyway ! This harm is mine, so let it be in my own part I won't be able to handle the realistic, I tell you to take her place and I'm not ordering you, I'm making a request... Just handle my family!VAIDIK : How have you ever seen a football match in your life?

__AYU__ : You can hide your truth with everyone, but you can't.

__VAIDIK__ : What do you mean what do you say? Age in the Just List I am being said. **"**

Why did you say that you know my truth undefined What do you know about me undefined That was enough like this between us, after that he had lost his life and was in such a confusion of which I was oblivious and even unaware why he said to me that after killing my family, you should take care now my academy and My team is yours, I don't even know their names, nor have I ever played football before and who is talking about the truth, undefined what they know about my past and who is right in my past The incident happened due to which my anger is also oblivious? The past was related to me, I used to say Sunna that incident was related to my past, which I did not even know and do I already know the age? Why didn't I do the lights? On my part? There are also such accidents where we are far away from it even after being close to our destination. Every wall of the academy used to be wasted so much that he could never be hard on his feet again, in the face of what confusion and duty have I missed the floor where the wind of pain is blowing on one side, and on the other side does not trust anyone. And why am I trusting her feet, with whom my meeting was only for two moments, why I felt like myself, why her shoes seemed true to me, now this is a reality To make your thinking known, you will have to suffer a little bit about the time frame for the next part.

> *"I am tied in a relationship whose happiness is also in my gathering has come as a show of helplessness.*
> *For reality i have urged for conquered reality to the god but accidently the god have stucked me in the complicated fake reality.*
> *No matter how clear what you say but when time comes his thinking also hides behind the innocent faces."*

IV
RELATION GONE COMPLICATED

It is said that there are some accidents in life which do not have any value, the dreams related to them cause trouble all the time. What was the reality of my past, what were the wishes of my past, why was it necessary for me to love them, I did not say anything for them, which is coming out as the silence of my part, why did I get from him and good faith inside the evidence I am not even aware of the way, why is he feeling like my own, what is the reality of both? And who is the true truth and which trust is undefined. I was about to become aware because the relief of the confusion in which I killed my own hatred was keeping me alive in my mind every time a new story of pain in the feeling of each moment. Said that now my academy and its players in your hands did not say that Sameer was my team Means become the captain of our academy because if he took the place then we would never win, I could not beat his bat even after saying that once on the right foot he helped me that too by separating from the male crowd and I had said this only at a time when you can remember me beyond my needs, I was unaware of my feet, I told myself that I had been informed that she was also an international player after seeing the love of two moments. Nor did I have any interest in the male football match, but I was forced to say that even after saying no, I challenged Sameer for the captaincy and the duty that Age had shown, I also tried to save my team. Time did it because it says undefined.

> **"The desire for revenge is fulfilled only when
> Enemy's affection
> and war are completely related."**

I know that a little work has been done for them at the time of hatred, my feet are not my love. I could always forget that before undefined male academy, I saw two advantages behind it.. first was that if I accidentally played male academy and that too as a captain, if I win the male match then all the trustees wa mine under already went on that time if I won the match I meant to say shish baat formula no ek teer seh do targeted the point and that if I give my academy a lot of heart in the match then maybe their hatred will turn into love and the trustees who were the trustees of the US academy would probably make me better. I thought it was a matter of respect for him too and it was a matter of respect, it was a matter of his academy first.. The second advantage was that I would not need to do anything, nor would I have to do anything in front of him by the traps of love and fury. Will not throw, nor listen to his unfaithful words, Pareg means code no" Direct entry into the enemy house"" .I already knew these things that the boys of the male academy don't like me very much and neither do half the teachers of the coven, so when I challenged Sameer, his coach told me to say that if you are in a school match If I go wrong then you will have to leave the academic academy I can't beat him even if he says, but he never gets any luck in the strength of which belong to the life of victory, everyone is a public, so there should also be brain capacity for him, which can balance both and win any battle. I also knew that if I miss the school match, I will have to leave the men's academy and my dreams, which brought the word of ruin, also against the sat john academy, they may never be fulfilled if I go to the men's academy. It was not only about my respect when I left and my mother had shed tears and my father brought her back again in the respect she had sung. I used to say that even if I had lost my time, maybe my love would have accepted the defeat, but that dream would never come true, nor did I ever miss the price of the death of my parents. Do not leave this is a golden opportunity for me, which I want in any way in my part I had a little work when I did the challenge, so I was one sided, that meant no one was with me, neither that academy nor any other leg like: We started our match against the other side that too in front of all Academy and it will complete In the academy, listen to the alphabets of only one name, that too for Fateh, which was also from Sameer Rathore. Aryabhatta's inventions were present, meaning zero, everyone had decided my troubles long ago, undefined, many people were saying this too, now I have gone where I don't even wear clothes. Let your loser undefined run away from the local undefined! And I needed this. Hate also had a different meaning, which takes us straight to the road of victory, which means that what was not supposed to happen, after all, the match happened even after half an hour had passed. What was the score of the foot next half hour? What these people say? Had taken the steps means Vaidik Verma non demo noob player had given every to an international player means Sameer Rathore had lost his captaincy! One day a reality and it came to the fore that hatred also accepts victory in prayer and my hatred Then was roaming everywhere in the words of victory, still wondered why age told me that I had to destroy his academy. I am undefined only I can handle his academy out, I can even win the match, my questions were still bothering me Even before I could find it in complete Academy, everyone had lifted me on their shoulders and started talking about such a celebration, as they know me from long ago, on this day another thing came before my eyes that of relationships in St John Academy. There is no cost, it is only that friend, whether it is their relationship, because the bonding of age was more than them, when he lost the match and no one supported his captaincy, then no one supported him. ayu supposed that the whole academic team as a family, he also left her side for a long time, he also lost her just for one fate, well I neither had to make new friends with him nor play him because my destination was very clear now because I Now it had come in the eyes of the trustees and Ridhi Kalra, who was not well known to me, was my life. the biggest success was I had forgotten that they say we can't win a match until the fielding is done, I didn't even know that she is the daughter of Head Trustee, that means daughter of Bajaj Kalra (Head Trustee of St John Academy undefined) .Means what I found in the complete gathering was the shift in my part I did not even think that whatever I am doing every day in prayer for God, it will unnecessarily come in my part. I was also aware that she is the daughter of Bajal Kalra, that means the enemy is sitting in my own grave and I do not even know about the matter, now that match was very important for me, I should give any progress to the National Unity Academy. Will have to defeat the field of Bajal Kalra because the daughter of Bajal Kalra had gone mad in my love, feet are still the grave of Bajal Kalra She was not ready and neither the day I defeated Sameer rathore of Usha Academy, the day she proposed me in front of complete Academy, foot she didn't know at all that she is the daughter of Bajaj Kalra. When I came to know about this, my happiness was absolutely the seventh heaven, that means now I have achieved all the blessings and the dreams that I had dreamed of destroying every one of the academy, they were soon going to turn into reality, he's the trustee of Then if it was related to me then it was the happiness and he was waiting for the thing in all the three groups of feet, that thing was not found till now, what will he get in my share in the future undefined and what will be the cost of my parents' father's son which Bajal Kalra's Because of undefined I will be able to carry forward the tradition of vengeance undefined as I will be able to destroy Bajal Kalra undefined and who is the real person related to my past and who brought me up are they my real parents undefined and who is the relationship I have added her, is she real, am I her blood? undefined what age before undefined If we have met before then why can't I remember those moments undefined and will I be able to make Riddhi Kalra's love a waste of my success and Bajaj Kalra's undefined where I too have fallen in love with her undefined after all What was my answer to express him on this day, what did I say to him after all? There are many undefined questions, the truth of the answer is not yet decided and the words of the time are not yet fulfilled, you will have to adopt the love of patience, because the story is still good, my friend! I have written my story in its entirety. It is a coincidence that my friends are incomplete, that too because of the past. Take it and try to live your life with the help of it, then it will never be accepted. And if you want to ruin someone's love, never defame someone's love, because one-sided love is not destined for everyone, it is hot and the matter of ruin is famous in those abuses of love where even the winds of pain would have been included in the word of deceit. Accidents are not eradicated by committing crimes, because with time their pain becomes deeper and every crime in the world is punished, if you cannot give happiness to someone for two moments in charity, then there is also a reason for sorrow in his gathering. dont made by the verma Neither the recommendation of pain will be left nor the smell of happiness in the fire. Feet, their characters remain incomplete, my story is also similar in which due to some moments of character then it will be realted to that past of strange The man is related to the past, which I do not know their love is incomplete undefined

"

*In this world if your relationship is much less
the hurtness will be very less
I have prayed that I have cried behind every
evidence with whom I have had such a deep
relationship.*

*Some of the relationship's goodness forced it to say
that we could also do it by chance and just by
chance,
today you have got happiness definitely, let the
time come,
if we have not wasted your family, we are not
even the sons of one father.* "

Jazmin

EDITION 1 IS ENDED HERE.